Space Dog in Trouble

by Natalie Standiford

illustrated by Kathleen Collins Howell

A STEPPING STONE BOOK™

Random House New York

www.randomhouse.com/kids

Library of Congress Cataloging-in-Publication Data
Standiford, Natalie.
Space Dog in trouble / by Natalie Standiford ; illustrated by Kathleen Collins
Howell. p. cm. "A Stepping Stone book." SUMMARY: When Roy and his parents
go away for the weekend, Space Dog, who is really an alien from the planet
Queekrg, is left on his own and gets picked up by a local animal rescue group.
ISBN 0-679-88905-1 (pbk.) — ISBN 0-679-98905-6 (lib. bdg.)
[1. Dogs—Fiction. 2. Extraterrestrial beings—Fiction]
I. Howell, Kathleen Collins, ill.
II. Title.   PZ7.S78627Spi 1999 [Fic]—dc21 97-27300

Printed in the United States of America 10 9 8 7 6 5 4 3 2 1

A STEPPING STONE BOOK is a trademark of Random House, Inc.

Contents

1

Space Dog and His Collar

It was late in the summer. School would start soon. Roy Barnes tried not to think about it. He thought about peanut butter instead.

He was in the kitchen trying to spell out ROY with peanut butter on a piece of bread. The letters were hard to read, so Roy finally gave up.

He made two sandwiches and put each of them on a plate. Then he took them out to the backyard.

Roy's dog, Space Dog, was in his dog-house. Roy knocked out the secret code on the door of the doghouse—two slow knocks and two fast. Space Dog said, "Come in, Roy."

Roy crawled in. The doghouse looked like an office inside. There was a desk and a computer. Space Dog worked in the dog-house. He was secretly studying the ways of Earth people.

Space Dog was a creature from outer space—the planet Queekrg, to be exact. His spaceship had crash-landed in Roy's backyard one night months before. Ever since that night, Roy and Space Dog had been best friends.

"Hi, Space Dog," said Roy. "How's your work going?"

"Pretty well," said Space Dog. He was typing on the computer. "I'm writing a report about Earth food. It's making me hungry."

"Good," said Roy. "I brought you a snack." He handed a plate to Space Dog.

Space Dog looked at the sandwich. "Could this be peanut butter?" he asked, peeking under the bread. "It is! Just what I was in the mood to eat!"

Roy bit into his sandwich, watching Space Dog. Space Dog looked exactly like an Earth dog. Roy's parents (and everyone else) thought Space Dog was just a regular dog. But he wasn't. He could walk on two legs like a person. He could talk and write. And he was very smart. When people were watching, Space Dog had to act like a dog. But when he was alone with Roy, he acted like a person. Suddenly Roy noticed something was missing.

"Hey," he said with a mouth full of

peanut butter. "Where's your collar?"

"You shouldn't talk with your mouth full," said Space Dog. Then he stuffed half his sandwich into his mouth.

Roy swallowed. "Why aren't you wearing your collar?" he said. "I keep telling you it's dangerous to go around without your dog tags. What if you got lost or something? I'd never find you."

Space Dog pointed to his mouth. He was trying to say that he couldn't talk because his mouth was full.

Roy waited impatiently for Space Dog to finish chewing. When Space Dog reached for the other half of his sandwich, Roy stopped him. "Don't stuff more food in your mouth!" said Roy. "You have to answer my question. Why aren't you wearing your collar?"

Space Dog sighed. "Because I hate it,"

he whined. "I feel like I'm choking."

"I know," said Roy. "But you have to wear it anyway. School starts soon, and I won't be around all day. You might need help when I'm not here."

"There's nothing to worry about," said Space Dog. "I'll be careful."

"Will you wear your collar?" said Roy.

"That collar is awful," Space Dog said. "It's like wearing a leather tie."

"Does that mean you won't promise?"

"That's right," said Space Dog.

"Sometimes you're such a pain!" said Roy. "If you were a regular dog, we wouldn't even be talking about this. I would just put your collar on, and it would stay there."

"I know," said Space Dog. "But I'm not a regular dog. If I were, you wouldn't have gotten an A in math last spring."

Roy had to admit Space Dog was right. Most dogs wouldn't have been able to tutor him in math.

"I'll promise you this," said Space Dog. "I'll wear the collar when you go back to school—but only when I leave the backyard."

"Okay," said Roy. "But until then, be careful."

"Don't worry," said Space Dog. "I've been all over the universe. I'm sure I can find my way around this neighborhood."

2
That's Life

"Guess what, Roy," said Mrs. Barnes at dinner that night. "We're going to Granny's this weekend."

Oh, no, thought Roy. *Now I'm in for it.*

Roy hated going to his grandmother's house. She made him wear a tie at dinner. She always told him he was holding his knife wrong or that he should be using a different fork.

"One thing, son," said Mr. Barnes. "Space Dog has to stay here."

Roy dropped his fork. "Why?" he said. "I want him to come with us."

"Granny doesn't like dogs," said Mrs. Barnes. "And you know she has those cats. I was thinking maybe Alice could come over and feed Space Dog while we're gone." Alice lived next door. She and Roy were friends.

"I could stay here with Space Dog," said Roy. "We'd be okay by ourselves."

"You can't stay here, and that's that," said Mr. Barnes. "Give Alice a call after dinner and see if she'll feed the dog."

"At least Alice won't have to walk Space Dog," said Mrs. Barnes. "He can use the dog door to go out back."

The dog door was something Roy's father had made. It was a little swinging door at the bottom of the back door. Space Dog could open and close the back door with no trouble at all, of course. But Mr. Barnes didn't know that.

Roy knew there was no way out of going to Granny's. After dinner he went up to his room and broke the news to Space Dog.

Space Dog didn't think it was bad news. "I'll get a lot of work done while you're gone," he said. "Alice doesn't have to come over and feed me. I can cook my own meals."

"No, you can't!" said Roy. "We don't want my parents to know you can cook."

"That's true," said Space Dog. "Well, Alice can come over and serve me dog food. After she leaves, I'll throw out the dog food and make a hamburger or something."

"What about the trash?" Roy said.

"Alice will see the dog food in the garbage."

"I'll clean up before Alice comes," said Space Dog. "I'll take the trash outside. Don't worry. I'll work it out."

Roy sat still for a minute. Space Dog flipped through a magazine.

Finally Roy said, "Aren't you even going to miss me?"

Space Dog closed the magazine. "Sure I am," he said. "But you won't be gone long. It's only a weekend."

"It always seems like forever at Granny's," said Roy. "That dumb Pesty!"

"Who's Pesty?"

"She's this girl who lives next door to Granny. Her real name is Marian. Granny makes me play with her. She follows me around. Mom says she's just lonely."

"I knew a kid like that once," said

Space Dog. "His name was Terg. He talked my ear off."

"That sounds just like Pesty," Roy said.

"He had to be the boss of everything. Nobody liked him. He always wanted to fly around in my toy spaceship. He kept asking and asking if he could drive it."

"You had your own spaceship when you were little?" said Roy. "Cool!"

"A lot of kids had them," said Space Dog. "Even Terg had one. But for some reason he always wanted to drive mine."

"What happened?" asked Roy.

"I finally let him," said Space Dog.

"Then what?" said Roy.

"He crashed my little spaceship into my parents' spaceship. We both got into big trouble."

"Wow," said Roy. "Thanks for telling me that story. Now I feel even *worse* about going to Granny's."

"At least Pesty doesn't live next door to *you*," said Space Dog. "Anyway, everybody has to have someone who's a pest. That's life."

3

Off to Granny's

On Friday morning, the Barneses got ready to go to Granny's. Roy was supposed to be packing, but he sat on his bed in a gloomy mood.

"Cheer up," said Space Dog. "Maybe Pesty will be away on vacation or something."

"I hope so," said Roy. "Will you be okay here?"

"I'll be fine," said Space Dog. "I'm looking forward to standing up and walking around on two feet again."

"Alice will be over to feed you this afternoon," said Roy. "Just remember you're a dog."

"I will," said Space Dog. "I like Alice. It's Blanche that bothers me." Blanche was Alice's poodle.

Mrs. Barnes called, "Roy! We're almost ready to leave. Bring your bag."

"I've got to go," Roy said. He hugged Space Dog.

"Have a good trip," said Space Dog.

"Don't answer the phone," said Roy. "And don't stand up in front of Alice."

"I won't," said Space Dog. "Bye."

"Bye."

Space Dog watched out the living room window as the Barneses drove away. When they were gone, he jumped off the sofa. "Hurray!" he said. "I have the whole

house to myself—at last!"

He ran straight to the kitchen and opened the refrigerator. "Hmm," he said. "Tomatoes, eggs, cheese. This looks like omelet fixings to me."

Soon Space Dog was eating a gooey omelet. Dirty pans and dishes were piled all over the kitchen. When he finished eating, Space Dog stretched out on the living room sofa for a nap. *I'll do the dishes later*, he thought drowsily. *Alice won't be here for hours*.

An hour later Alice opened the door to Roy's house with the key Mr. Barnes had given her. Alice had Blanche with her. She knew Space Dog didn't like her dog, but she kept hoping he would change his mind. Poor Blanche. She loved Space Dog so.

Alice and Blanche went into the house.

Space Dog was still lying on the couch in the living room. Blanche ran right to him and licked his face. Space Dog's eyes were closed, but he was almost awake. *Help! I'm drowning in slime!* he thought.

Space Dog opened his eyes. Blanche was nose to nose with him. He jumped off the couch in fright. Luckily he landed on all fours.

Alice saw what happened. "Oh, Space Dog," she said. "Blanche won't hurt you. She's just trying to be friends."

Space Dog stopped himself from answering. He backed away from Blanche and ran upstairs. Alone at last, he washed the slime off his face.

"Come back, Space Dog!" Alice called from downstairs. "It's food time."

As Space Dog dried his face, he told himself he had to try to be a real dog for

Alice. He forced himself to go back downstairs. Alice patted him and said, "Good boy!" Then she went to the kitchen.

"What a mess!" she said when she saw all the dirty dishes. "Mr. and Mrs. Barnes didn't even bother to clean the kitchen before they left."

She opened the cookie jar and treated herself to a cookie. Then she looked around for the dog food. "I wonder where they keep it?" she said.

I hope she doesn't find it, thought Space Dog.

"Oh, here it is," said Alice. She pulled a can from one of the cupboards. Blanche knew it was dog food. She began to drool.

"No, Blanche, you eat later," said Alice. "This is Space Dog's food." She opened the can of dog food, and the smell floated toward Space Dog. He turned his head away. He hated dog food with all his heart.

"Where's your bowl, Space Dog?" asked Alice.

Space Dog didn't move. He didn't have a dog-food bowl. He didn't want a dog-food bowl. He just wanted Alice and Blanche to go home.

Alice picked out a bowl and said, "This will do, I guess." She plopped the dog food into the bowl. "Here you go, boy," she said to Space Dog. "Chow time!"

Blanche trotted over to the bowl. "No, Blanche, no!" said Alice. "That's not for you."

Alice held Blanche by the collar and waited for Space Dog to start eating. "Aren't you hungry, Space Dog?" she said.

Space Dog just sat there. He didn't want to hurt Alice's feelings, but he was not going to eat the brown glop. He could

only go so far with this dog business.

Blanche began to pull away from Alice's hold. She wanted the dog food.

"Blanche, you're a bad girl," said Alice. "I'd better take you home." She dragged Blanche out the door, calling back over her shoulder, "Bye, Space Dog. See you tomorrow."

As soon as Alice was gone, Space Dog emptied the dog food into the garbage. Then he fixed himself a sandwich of ham on rye.

4

A Terrible Thing Happens

That night Space Dog watched horror movies on TV and ate corn chips. He stayed up late and had a good time, but he would have had more fun if Roy had been there.

Saturday morning Space Dog woke up to face even more dirty dishes than the day before. He began washing them. Then he stopped.

I can't wash the dishes, he thought to himself. *Alice has seen the mess in the kitchen. If everything is clean all of a sudden, she'll wonder what's going on.*

Space Dog decided not to clean the kitchen until the next day, Sunday, just before the Barneses were supposed to get home.

Alice didn't bring Blanche with her when she came over to feed Space Dog on Saturday afternoon. When she walked into the kitchen, Alice said, "This place looks messier than yesterday! But it couldn't be…"

Alice couldn't figure out what had happened. Finally she checked the dog-food bowl and said, "Good boy, Space Dog! You ate everything I gave you. Ready for more?"

Space Dog hung his head.

Alice opened another can of dog food and spooned it into the bowl. Then she set the bowl down and patted Space Dog. "I would stay and keep you company," she said, "but I have to go play softball. See you later!" And she ran out the door.

Space Dog put the dog food in a plastic bag and buried it in the trash. Then he fixed himself some ice cream. *There's nothing like a nice cold lunch to get you through the day*, he thought to himself. Then he ducked through the dog door and went outside.

Space Dog was busy in his doghouse with a report on horror movies when he heard a creepy sniffing, slurping sound. He froze.

The sound seemed to be coming closer. *Sniff, slurp.*

What is that? thought Space Dog. *Do I dare go outside and check?*

Space Dog remembered the horror

movies he had seen the night before. There were giant blobs that swallowed people. Huge lizards with thousands of teeth.

Get ahold of yourself, thought Space Dog. *There are no blobs out there. There are no lizards.*

Space Dog heard breathing. *Sniff. Slurp.* He forced himself to open the door of the doghouse a little way.

It was Blanche! She was standing right by the door of the doghouse. Suddenly she started licking Space Dog's face. Slobber flew everywhere.

Space Dog had to get away. He ran in a circle around the yard. When Blanche followed, Space Dog jumped the back fence and ran down the street.

Blanche followed close behind Space Dog, leaving a trail of drool. Space Dog checked again and again to see where she was. Finally Blanche slowed down a little. She seemed to be giving up the chase. Space Dog looked back one more time…

Suddenly he bumped into someone. It was a man in a dark blue uniform.

"Gotcha!" said the man. He grabbed Space Dog. "No dogs allowed on the street without a leash. And what's this?" He felt around Space Dog's furry neck. "No collar? No tags? A stray! You're coming with me, Fido."

He picked Space Dog up. Space Dog struggled, but the man was strong. He carried Space Dog toward a small truck. On the side of the truck were the words SAVE-A-STRAY ANIMAL SHELTER.

Oh, no! thought Space Dog. *This is just what Roy warned me about!*

"In you go!" said the dog warden. He

set Space Dog down in the back of the truck and then slammed the rear doors closed.

Space Dog stared out the barred window. *Help! I'm a prisoner!* he cried silently. As the truck drove away, he saw Blanche

chasing it. But the truck was going too fast. Blanche had to give up. Space Dog watched her fade in the distance.

The dog warden's truck stopped at a small, low building. There was a sign in front that said SAVE-A-STRAY ANIMAL SHELTER. The dog warden got out of the truck, pulled Space Dog out of the back, and carried him into the building.

I can't believe this is happening, thought Space Dog. He wished he could talk to someone. But he remembered what Roy had once told him about talking to Earth people. "When they find out where you're from," Roy had said, "they'll take you to a lab and study you. They might even take your brain apart."

Space Dog knew Roy was right. He had to think of a way out of this without talking to anyone. He couldn't give his secret away.

The warden took Space Dog into an office. "Here's another one, Smiley," he said to a gray-haired man in a white coat. He put Space Dog down on a metal table and left the office. Space Dog was alone with Smiley.

"Hi there, fella," the man in the white coat said to Space Dog. He patted him. "I'm just going to check you out a little bit."

Space Dog realized that Smiley was a dog doctor and that he was about to have a checkup. *He's in for a shock if he checks my blood*, Space Dog thought nervously. Space Dog's blood was not the normal Earth kind. It was bright blue.

Space Dog was lucky. Smiley didn't check his blood. He just looked him over carefully and said, "You're a little over-weight but fit as a fiddle." Then he led Space Dog down a hallway to a big room full of dogs in cages. Smiley put Space Dog in a cage and said, "See you at sup-pertime!"

Space Dog looked around. His cage was small and hot. There were cages on both sides and across the way. The dogs in the other cages scratched and whined and barked. The noise was awful. *This is terri-ble*, thought Space Dog. *How am I ever going to get out of here?*

In the cage to his left, Space Dog could see a long-eared, flea-bitten hound. The hound did nothing but sit and scratch, scratch, scratch. On Space Dog's right was a little poodle puppy. It jumped around its cage and yipped nonstop.

Space Dog tried to open the door of

his cage, but it had been locked with a key. There was nothing to do but sit. *I wish they'd give us something to read*, he thought. He was beginning to itch. He had already caught the hound's fleas.

After a while two people came into the room. One was a staff member and the other was a little old lady. "I'm looking for a nice dog to keep me company," said the lady.

"We've got plenty of those," the staff man answered.

The old lady walked through the room. She looked in every cage. As she passed, dogs stuck their noses through the bars and whined.

The old lady stopped at Space Dog's cage. "What about this one?" she said.

"He's not up for adoption yet," the man said. "We just got him in today. No

adoption for the first twenty-four hours."

Adoption? thought Space Dog. *What is he talking about?*

Then the old lady looked at the poodle puppy. The puppy wagged its tail and held out its paw to the old lady.

Look at that silly puppy, thought Space Dog. *He's just trying to be cute. Yuck!*

"Look at this darling puppy!" said the old lady. She shook his paw. "He's adorable. Could you open his cage?"

This woman obviously has no taste, thought Space Dog.

"I think I'll take this one," said the lady when she had the puppy cuddled in her arms.

"Sure thing," said the staff man. "This way." The three of them left the room.

Hold it right there! thought Space Dog. *I get it! People come here to adopt strays. Then they take their new pets home. Well, that's how I'll get out of here!*

Space Dog decided to be as cute as pie for the first person who came the next day. In the meantime, he was hungry. It was time for supper, and Smiley reappeared. All the dogs began to bark. Smiley put a tin of dog food into each cage.

I don't believe it, thought Space Dog, staring at his supper. *This looks worse than the dog food Alice gave me.*

Space Dog pushed the dog food into a corner of his cage and listened to his stomach rumble. He decided to try to sleep. *Maybe that will help me forget how hungry I am*, he thought.

The other dogs wolfed down their food. Space Dog scratched and remembered his comfortable bed at Roy's house. *I miss Roy*, he thought. *He takes good care of me. If I had listened to Roy and worn my collar, I wouldn't be in this mess!*

Space Dog gave his ear another scratch, curled up, and tried to sleep.

5

Roy Comes Home

It was Sunday at last. Roy sat quietly in the back seat of his parents' car. They were on their way home from Granny's.

The weekend had been pretty bad. Pesty had a broken ankle and had to stay at home. Granny told Roy to go over and keep her company on Saturday afternoon.

Roy went, but he didn't want to. While he was there, he asked Pesty if he could try her crutches. She said no, he couldn't. Roy tried them anyway, and

Pesty started to cry.

In the end Roy had to say he was sorry to everybody. He was glad when the weekend was over. He had worried about Space Dog the whole time. He hoped nothing bad had happened to him.

At last the car pulled into the Barneses' driveway. "Home again!" said Mr. Barnes. He was in a jolly mood. Roy got out of the car and ran to the front door of the house. It was locked, of course, so he waited for his parents to catch up and open the door.

As soon as it was open, Roy ran inside and called, "Space Dog! We're home!" But there was no answer. Space Dog did not appear.

Roy walked into the kitchen, calling for Space Dog. Then he saw the mess there, with dirty dishes everywhere. Roy panicked. *Oh, no!* he thought. *Space Dog didn't clean up!*

Mrs. Barnes was right behind Roy. "What happened in here?" she said. "I left the kitchen clean. Could Alice have done this?"

"Yeah," said Roy. "That's it. It was Alice."

"I don't think so," said his mother. "I think someone broke in while we were gone! Barney!" she called to Mr. Barnes. "Come here, quick!"

While his parents were in the kitchen, Roy went out back. *Space Dog must be in his doghouse*, he said to himself.

"Space Dog, I'm home!" he called. The doghouse door was open. *That's strange*, thought Roy. He stuck his head inside and looked around. No Space Dog.

Maybe he's upstairs asleep in my room,

thought Roy. He went back inside. His parents were checking to see if anything had been stolen.

"This is the strangest thing I ever heard of," said Mr. Barnes. "Why would someone break in just to mess up the kitchen?"

"I'll call Alice to see what she knows about it," said Mrs. Barnes. She went to the telephone and dialed Alice's number.

Roy ran upstairs. "Space Dog!" he called. He checked his room. He checked all the other rooms. There was no sign of Space Dog.

Roy ran back downstairs, yelling, "Mom! Dad! Space Dog is gone! He's really gone!"

"He must be around somewhere," said Mrs. Barnes. "Did you check the dog-house?"

"He's not there!" said Roy. "He's gone!"

Just then the doorbell rang. "That must

be Alice," said Mrs. Barnes. "I asked her to come over."

Mrs. Barnes went and got Alice and brought her into the kitchen.

"Do you know anything about these dirty dishes, Alice?" asked Mr. Barnes.

"They were here when I came in to feed Space Dog on Friday," said Alice. "I thought you left them."

"Forget about the dishes, Alice," said Roy. "Where's Space Dog?"

"I don't know," said Alice. "He was here yesterday afternoon when I came to feed him. I don't know what happened after that. You said I didn't have to come today because you would be home."

"Maybe someone stole him!" said Mr. Barnes. "Someone must have broken into the house, cooked a big meal, and then stolen our dog!" He picked up the phone and said, "Operator, get me the police."

Roy sat down and started to cry. "What if he's gone?" he said, sniffling. "What if he flew away?"

"Flew away?" said Alice. "Don't you mean *ran* away?"

Roy sniffed and nodded.

"Space Dog would never run away," said Mrs. Barnes. "He loves you too much."

"But if he didn't run away," said Roy, "where is he?"

Soon two police officers arrived to make a report. Mr. Barnes told them everything.

"Let me see if I've got this straight," said one police officer. "You say someone broke into your house, cooked a big meal, and stole your dog?"

"That's right," said Mr. Barnes.

"And nothing else is missing?"

"Nothing," said Mrs. Barnes. "Our silver-ware was right out in plain sight, and it's all still there."

"Very strange," said the officer. "Do you mind if we look around?"

"Not at all," said Mr. Barnes.

The two officers checked all through

the house. "No sign of a break-in," one of the officers said. "Did you call the dog pound? They might have your dog."

"We'll call right now," said Mrs. Barnes. She looked up the number and dialed. But it was too late. By the time she called, Space Dog was gone.

6

Space Dog's New Home

Space Dog had spent a noisy, itchy Saturday night at the shelter. By Sunday morning, he was hungrier than ever. But there was still nothing to eat but dog food.

I've got to get out of here, he thought. *Think, brain, think! What should I do?*

The answer soon arrived. That afternoon, as Roy and his parents were driving home from Granny's, a family came into the animal shelter. It was a young couple with three-year-old twins. Their name was

Cranston.

"We're looking for a sweet dog for our children," the mother explained at the front desk.

The staff person led the Cranston family into the room full of cages. "Somewhere in this room," said the staffer, "is the pet you're looking for."

The dogs stood up and began to bark. But not Space Dog. He studied the Cranston family closely. Mr. and Mrs. Cranston were well dressed. The twins—a boy and a girl—were small, chubby blonds with a little bit of leftover chocolate on their faces.

Space Dog decided the Cranstons would go for a cute dog. He went into his best cuddly act. He opened his eyes as wide as he could and looked sad.

When the twins came to his cage, he

stuck out his paw the way the poodle puppy had done. But the twins didn't shake his paw. They just stared at him.

I have to make them want to adopt me, Space Dog said to himself. The little girl's face was close to the bars of his cage. Space Dog stuck his head through the bars as far as he could and licked the chocolate off the little girl's face.

The girl giggled and laughed. "Mommy!" she cried. "I want this doggy!"

"Me, too," said the little boy.

The parents looked at Space Dog.

"You want *this* one?" said Mr. Cranston. "He looks a little strange."

"Wouldn't you rather have a sweet little puppy?" asked Mrs. Cranston.

"No!" said the little girl. "I want *this* doggy!"

"Are you *sure?*" asked her mother.

"Yes! Yes!" both children cried.

"Okay," said Mr. Cranston. "We'll take this one."

Hurray! Space Dog shouted to himself. *I'm out of here at last. Now all I have to do is find my way back to Roy's.*

The staff person unlocked Space Dog's cage and led him out of the room. Before long, he belonged to the Cranstons, and they all headed home.

Space Dog sat in the back of the Cranstons' station wagon. The car windows were open, and the wind blew through Space Dog's fur. *Ah*, he thought. *Fresh air! Freedom!*

The children turned around in their seats to pat their new dog. "My name is Buffy," said the little girl.

"My name is Floyd," said the little boy.

Pleased to know you, thought Space Dog. *For a little while, anyway.*

"Well, kids," said Mrs. Cranston. "What shall we name your new dog?"

"Buffy!" said Buffy.

Floyd frowned. "No, not Buffy!" he said. "Floyd! His name is Floyd."

It's bad enough being called Space Dog, thought Space Dog. *But Buffy and Floyd are out of the question.*

"Buffy!" screamed Buffy.

"Floyd!" screamed Floyd.

"Buffy!" yelled Buffy. And she hit Floyd.

"Stop!" said Floyd. And he hit Buffy back.

Space Dog covered his ears.

"Stop, both of you!" said Mr. Cranston. "Or we'll turn around and take the dog back!"

Buffy and Floyd didn't make another sound.

"That's better," said their father.

"I have an idea," said Mrs. Cranston. "Let's name the dog Fluffy. The first two letters, *F* and *L*, are from Floyd, and the *uffy* is from Buffy. That way the dog's name comes from both your names!"

Fluffy? thought Space Dog. *Oh, brother.*

The station wagon pulled into a drive-way. "Here we are, Fluffy!" said Mrs. Cranston. "Your new home."

Space Dog looked out the window at a small brick house. He had never seen it before. *I wonder if this is anywhere near Roy's house,* he thought to himself.

"We're ready for you, Fluffy," said Mr. Cranston. "I've got a new collar and a leash and a house full of dog food."

Mr. Cranston got out of the front seat and opened the back door of the station wagon. He put the collar around Space Dog's neck and then hooked the leash to it.

There's no escaping right now, thought Space Dog. *I'll have to watch for my chance.*

The Cranstons led Space Dog to the

backyard. Mr. Cranston unsnapped the leash. Then he tied a rope to Space Dog's collar. The rope was attached to a stake in the ground.

"That should hold him for now," said Mr. Cranston. "I've used my strongest navy knots. After all, we don't want Fluffy getting loose."

"Mommy, can Fluffy sleep with me?" asked Buffy.

"I want Fluffy to sleep with me!" said Floyd.

"He's not going to sleep with anyone," said Mrs. Cranston. "He's going to stay outside while the weather is nice."

What? thought Space Dog in alarm. *If I'm tied outside, that means I can't get to a telephone to call Roy. And I can't run away and try to find my way back to his house!*

"Come on inside, kids," said Mr.

Cranston. "Let's get some food for Fluffy."

Space Dog's stomach growled. He hadn't eaten since the day before. But he knew that the Cranstons would bring him dog food. *I'll starve to death if I don't get to Roy's soon*, he thought.

Mr. Cranston returned with a bowl of dog food. Buffy and Floyd toddled after him, eating big chocolate-chip cookies.

Mr. Cranston put the food in front of Space Dog. "Here you go, Fluffy."

Space Dog didn't move.

"That's funny," said Mr. Cranston. "He's not eating. Oh, well. Maybe it's because everything is so new. I'm going inside now, kids. You two can stay out here and play with Fluffy. Your mother will be out in a couple of minutes." And he marched inside the house.

The twins patted Space Dog and took

bites out of their big cookies. Space Dog looked at the cookies, and his mouth began watering. Suddenly he turned and licked Buffy's cookie.

"Eeeww!" cried Buffy. "Fluffy licked my cookie." She dropped it on the grass and ran toward the house.

Then Space Dog reached over and licked Floyd's cookie. "Mommy! Mommy!" cried Floyd. "The doggy licked *my* cookie!"

Mrs. Cranston came outside. "Don't eat those cookies, kids!" she said. "They have dog germs on them."

Mrs. Cranston went back in the house and brought out new cookies for Buffy and Floyd. "Don't stand next to Fluffy while you eat them," she warned. Then the phone rang. Mrs. Cranston ran inside again, calling, "I'll be right back, kids!"

As soon as she was gone, Space Dog

picked up the cookies that the children had dropped and gobbled them down. The twins watched him while they nibbled on their new cookies.

When they finished eating, the two children began playing with Space Dog. Buffy patted him on the nose. Floyd pulled his tail and said, "Honk, honk!"

Space Dog was friendly and didn't growl, so the twins grew braver. Buffy climbed up on his back and said, "Go, horsey, go!"

Buffy waited, but Space Dog didn't move. "Go, horsey!" Buffy said again. She pulled Space Dog's fur.

Ouch! thought Space Dog. *That hurts!*

"Honk!" Floyd pulled his tail again.

I can't stand much more of this, Space Dog thought sadly. *Roy, oh, Roy, where are you?*

7

Blanche Saves the Day

Roy couldn't sit still. He was very worried about Space Dog. He had just checked the basement. Space Dog's spaceship was still hidden there, so he knew Space Dog had not flown back to Queekrg. But where could he be?

Roy's parents had driven to the dog pound an hour earlier, but they hadn't found Space Dog there. Roy had gone to some of the neighbors' houses, but nobody had seen Space Dog. Alice had come by and was sitting on the front steps with Roy.

"It doesn't help to worry," said Alice. "Besides, we'll think of something."

She noticed Blanche lying at her feet, looking droopy. Blanche seemed to miss Space Dog, too.

"Look," said Alice. "Even Blanche is sad. Both of you are just moping around."

"I'm sorry," said Roy. "I can't help it. You don't understand."

"Yes, I do," Alice said. "You're worried about your dog."

"It's not just that," said Roy. "Space Dog is different. He's...special."

"Sure he's special," said Alice. "So is Blanche."

"That's not what I mean," said Roy. He moved closer to Alice on the steps. "Listen, if I tell you a secret, do you *promise* not to tell anybody?"

"Sure," said Alice. "What is it?"

"It sounds crazy," Roy said. "But—oh, never mind."

"You can't back down now!" said Alice. "You have to tell me. What's the secret?"

"Okay," said Roy. "Do you know why Space Dog is called Space Dog?"

"Why?"

"Because he's from outer space."

Alice stared at Roy for a second. Then she burst out laughing.

"It's not funny!" said Roy. "It's true!"

"Come on, Roy," said Alice. "You're making it up."

"I am not!" Roy said. "I'll prove it to you if we ever find Space Dog. I'll get him to talk. Then you'll believe me. Space Dog looks like a dog, but he's really a person."

"Sure he is. He's a person who won

first prize last month as Cutest Dog in a pet show."

"I'm telling the truth!" said Roy. "Have I ever lied to you?"

Alice thought for a minute. "No," she said. "You've never lied to me. But this is really weird. And anyway, why are you keeping it a secret if it's true?"

"To protect Space Dog," said Roy. "He's on a secret mission to Earth. Besides, if people find out he's an alien, they'll take him away to study him."

Alice stared at Roy. "You really believe all this stuff, don't you?" she said.

"Of course!" said Roy. "I'm telling you the truth! If Space Dog ever comes back, I'll make him talk to you. Then you'll feel really stupid for not believing me."

"Okay, okay," said Alice. "But how are we going to find him?"

"I don't know," said Roy. "We've already walked all over the neighborhood. My parents checked the dog pound. They put an ad in the paper. What else can we do?"

Just then Blanche sat up. Her ears twitched. She sniffed the air. She seemed very excited.

"What's she doing?" asked Roy.

"I don't know," said Alice. "She smells something."

Blanche ran down the front walk and headed down the street past Alice's house. Alice and Roy chased after her. Blanche finally came to a stop three houses away. She was barking at something in a tree.

"It's just a cat," said Alice when she and Roy caught up with Blanche. "Blanche is always chasing cats."

Roy looked thoughtful. "That's pretty amazing," he said. "She smelled the cat from three houses away."

"Sure," said Alice. "She can smell a lot better than we can. She can smell me coming home from school a block away."

"I've got an idea!" said Roy. "Blanche is in love with Space Dog, right?"

"Right," said Alice.

"And whenever he's around, she goes straight to him, right?"

"Right."

"So if we walk her all over the neighborhood, maybe she can smell Space Dog!" said Roy.

"That's a good idea!" said Alice. "Give her something to sniff first, something that has Space Dog's smell on it. What do you have that smells like him?"

"The pillowcase he was using, I guess," said Roy. "I haven't changed his sheets in a week."

"Changed his sheets?" Alice said. "You mean he sleeps in a bed?"

"Of course," said Roy. "I told you, he's just like a person."

"Roy," said Alice, "you're really getting weird."

Alice put Blanche's leash on and walked her back to Roy's house. Roy ran on ahead. He went into the house to get the pillowcase.

Roy brought the pillowcase back outside and stuck it under Blanche's nose. "Smell that, Blanche?" he said. "It's Space Dog!"

Blanche sniffed. She sniffed again. Then drool began to drip out of her mouth.

"Find him, girl!" said Alice.

Blanche started down the sidewalk. Roy and Alice followed her. She didn't seem to be picking up a scent, but she kept going. They crossed the street, and Blanche walked and walked. Every few blocks Roy held the pillowcase under her nose.

They walked a long way. Finally Alice and Roy were on a block they'd never seen before.

"We've gone pretty far," said Alice. "Maybe we should go back."

"Not yet," said Roy. "Just a few more blocks."

All at once Blanche pricked up her ears and began to sniff the air.

"She smells something!" said Roy.

"I hope it's not another cat," said Alice.

Blanche pulled at her leash. She wanted to run. Alice and Roy tried to run with her, but they couldn't keep up. Finally Alice let go of the leash.

Blanche raced ahead. She turned into a driveway and ran across a yard. Roy and Alice followed as fast as they could.

In the Cranstons' backyard, the twins were still pestering Space Dog. He tried to walk away, but the rope didn't let him go very

far. Space Dog needed a miracle.

And then there *was* a miracle. Space Dog suddenly saw something familiar come flying around the corner of the house. It looked like Blanche—and she was headed straight for him!

I don't believe it! Space Dog said to

himself. *I never thought I would be happy to see Blanche!*

The big poodle bounded up to Space Dog and licked his face. *Ugh!* thought Space Dog. *I'm not* that *happy to see you!*

Buffy and Floyd began to scream, "A new doggy! A new doggy!"

Mr. and Mrs. Cranston heard the noise. They rushed outside to see what was going on.

Just then Roy and Alice came panting around the corner after Blanche.

"Space Dog!" cried Roy. He ran and threw his arms around his furry pal. "We found you!"

The Cranstons stared at Roy in surprise. "Young man," said Mr. Cranston. "What are you doing here?"

Roy stood up. "My name is Roy Barnes, sir," he said. "And this is my friend Alice.

We've been looking all over town for my dog—and here he is!"

Mr. and Mrs. Cranston looked at each other.

"This is *your* dog?" said Mrs. Cranston.

Roy nodded.

"Are you sure?" said Mr. Cranston.

"I could call my parents and ask them to come over," said Roy. "They would tell you it's my dog."

"I guess there's been a mistake," said Mrs. Cranston. "You see, we adopted him from the Save-A-Stray Animal Shelter."

"Well, I'm not sure how he got to the shelter," said Roy. "But I know he's my dog. I wasn't home this weekend. I guess he got out of the yard."

"You should keep him tied up, like we do," said Mr. Cranston.

"Yes, sir," said Roy. He looked at Space

Dog. Space Dog stared back with a look that said, *Just try it, Roy!*

The Cranstons invited Roy and Alice inside the house so Roy could call home. His mother drove over in the car and identified Space Dog. Finally the Cranstons agreed that Space Dog should go home with Roy.

The twins didn't want Space Dog to go. Mrs. Cranston promised that she would take them back to the animal shelter the very next day so they could choose a new dog.

"This time we'll call him Buffy," said Buffy.

"We will not!" said Floyd. "We'll call him Floyd!"

The twins were still arguing as Mrs. Barnes drove away.

8

It's Good to Be Home

When they pulled into the driveway, Mr. Barnes was waiting to greet them.

"Welcome home, pooch," he said, giving Space Dog a pat. Then he and Mrs. Barnes went inside. Space Dog sat on the front steps with Roy and Alice.

"I'm so glad you're home, Space Dog!" said Roy. "But how did you end up at the animal shelter?"

Space Dog didn't answer. He wasn't going to talk to Roy as long as Alice was there.

Roy read Space Dog's mind. "It's okay, Space Dog," he said. "I told Alice all about you. You can talk in front of her. She won't tell."

Alice watched with interest. But Space Dog still didn't talk.

"Come on, Space Dog," said Roy. "Say something!"

Space Dog didn't open his mouth.

"It's okay, Roy," said Alice. "That stuff you told me about Space Dog...you were just upset then. He's back now, safe and sound."

"But—" said Roy.

"Space Dog is a dog," said Alice. "And dogs don't talk. Blanche doesn't talk, and Space Dog doesn't either."

"But—"

"Blanche and I are going home now," said Alice. "It's almost suppertime. See you later." Alice turned around and walked toward home with Blanche.

"Wait!" called Roy. "He really *can* talk! I'll prove it!"

Alice looked back and waved. Then she and Blanche went inside her house.

Roy glared at Space Dog. "Why didn't you talk?" he said. "Now Alice thinks I'm crazy!"

"I'm sorry, Roy," said Space Dog. "But I don't think Alice should know about me. You were right all along. I have to be very careful about what I say and what I do on this planet."

Then Space Dog told Roy the whole story. He told him about the animal shelter and the Cranstons. When he had finished, Space Dog said, "From now on, Roy, I'm going to wear my collar. I sure did miss you while you were gone."

"I missed you, too," said Roy. "When I got back and you weren't here, I was afraid I'd never see you again!"

"Before I went to the shelter, I didn't know how lucky I was," said Space Dog. "What if I had crashed in the Cranstons' backyard? My name would be Fluffy. I would be stealing cookies from little kids. And I wouldn't have a friend like you."

Roy hugged Space Dog. "I'm so glad you live at *my* house," he said.

Space Dog looked around. No one was watching, so he hugged Roy back. Then they heard a funny noise. *Grrrr.*

"What was that?" said Roy.

"That was my stomach growling," said Space Dog. "I'm starving. Would you please go inside and make me a little snack? About twenty peanut butter sandwiches ought to do it."

Roy smiled and went inside with Space Dog.

He made peanut butter sandwiches until his arm got tired. Space Dog ate them with a happy smack of his lips.

Then he said, with his mouth full, "It's good to be home."

It's a dog's life on earth!
But Space Dog puts up with it for his
new best friend, a human boy called Roy.

SPACE DOG AND ROY

When a spaceship crashes in his backyard, Roy gets what he's always wanted—a dog of his very own!

SPACE DOG AND THE PET SHOW

Space Dog agrees to enter a pet show for Roy's sake. But he didn't bargain on a beauty makeover at Dottie's Dog Salon!

SPACE DOG IN TROUBLE

A weekend at Granny's for Roy and his parents means a vacation for Space Dog—until he's dog-napped by the dogcatcher!

SPACE DOG THE HERO

Roy's dad insists that Space Dog guard the house. But Space Dog is a hopeless watchdog—he can't even growl!

About the Author

NATALIE STANDIFORD has often wondered if animals aren't secretly smarter than we think they are. She's sure that *kids* know a lot more than adults think they do. When she wrote about Space Dog, she imagined that he'd feel the way a lot of kids feel—misunderstood.

Natalie has written several books about dogs, but at home in New York City she has a cat, Iggy. So far, Iggy hasn't inspired any books. But you never know...

About the Illustrator

KATHLEEN COLLINS HOWELL began drawing pictures at age four and went on to study art in college. Today she is an illustrator of many books for children.

Kathleen and her husband, Jack, live half the year in Buffalo, New York, and half the year in rural England.